Tickly Prickly

by Bonny Becker · illustrated by Shari Halpern

HarperFestival®
A Division of HarperCollinsPublishers

Did you ever have a ladybug crawl across your finger?
How did it feel?
Tickly, prickly. Fly away quickly.

Did you ever have a moth brush your cheek?
How did it feel?
Whisper fluttery. Softly shuddery.

Did you ever have a lamb nudge
your fingers?
How did it feel?
Crinkly curls. Woolly whirls.

Did you ever have a chick nestle in your lap?
How did it feel?
Puffy. Peeping. Fluffy. Sleeping.

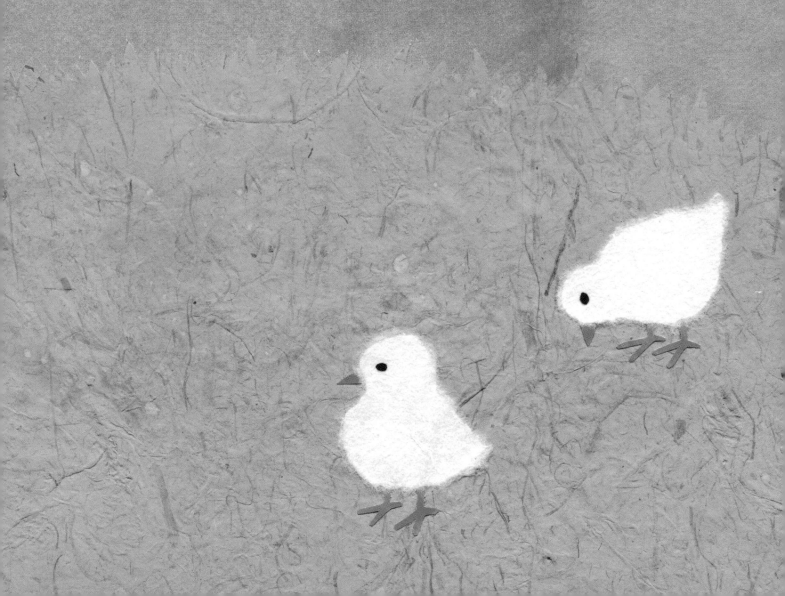

Did you ever have a cat pat your leg?
How did it feel?
Soft paw. Sharp claw.

Did you ever have a fish wriggle in your hands?
How did it feel?
Slippery, slickery. Turny and twistery.

Did you ever have a horse snort near
your ear?
How did it feel?
Moisty, musty. Warm and gusty.

Did you ever have a toad plop on your foot?
How did it feel?
Muddy, bumpy. Warty, lumpy.

Did you ever have a bunny nibble from your palm?
How did it feel?
Whiskery, shivery. Nose a-quivery.

Did you ever have a puppy cuddle
in your arms?
How did it feel?
Velvety snug. A hugful of love.